For Conner, Austin and Ethan

Chapter One

My name is Lark Ba, and I have my head in the clouds. Well, not really. If I had my head in the clouds, I'd be as big as a giant! That would be neat, though, because I'd *finally* be taller than my brother, Connor. He's my *little* brother, and he's *way* younger than me.

Having my head in the clouds is something my *halmoni*—that's Korean for *grandmother*—says when I start

1

daydreaming and get ~~distrackTed~~, ~~distracktid~~, distracted. I am trying hard to concentrate, only it is difficult because Connor and I are in a play, and I'm so excited!

The ~~kmunity~~, ~~cahmounity~~, community theater is doing *Alice in Wonderland*, and both Connor and I got parts! He gets to be a tree and the White Rabbit. I get to be the Caterpillar and one of the flowers. Plus, we each have talking parts. Pluser, I get to do more talking than Connor. That part is the bestest!

Being in a play means practicing very, very hard to memorize our lines. Connor and I were in the basement of our house. We had to be very, very quiet because it was early in the morning and we'd get in trouble if we woke up Mom, Dad or Halmoni. I sat on the couch with Max, our dog. Connor stood in front of us. "Connor, you're doing it wrong," I said.

He scowled. "No, I'm not."

Ugh. Little brothers. "Yes, you are. You're just standing there!"

"Lark, I'm a tree. I'm being a very good tree." To prove it, he stood with his feet wide apart and lifted his hands to the sky. "See? That's a tree."

"That's a stump with some branches. You're a tree! You have to look like it!"

He dropped his hands and backed away. "No! No way! You're not painting my face green with that sticky makeup again! I still have some behind my ears, and it's been two days."

I sighed. "I'm not talking about face paint. I'm talking about being a tree. They don't just stand there. They move if there's a breeze. Look at me." I stood with my feet wide apart and raised my arms. Then I wiggled my fingers and swayed my arms from side to side. "Like this."

"But there's nothing in the script about a breeze," he said.

"You're an actor. You're supposed to use your imagination and pretend big things. You should listen to me. After all, I'm older—"

"You are not!"

"—much older—"

"Twins, Lark, we're twins! And you're only older by ten minutes!"

"You should still listen to me because it's a good idea."

Connor folded his arms. "Okay. I can wave my hands around and pretend there's a breeze. But I need a break. Let's practice your part."

"I was practicing all last night, in bed."

"I know," said Connor. "I have the bunk underneath yours. And you're loud, even when you're trying to be quiet."

I decided to ignore what he said and to be patient, because I'm a very good big sister. I know I am. So does Connor, because I tell him that all the time.

"Let's take it from the top," he said.

That was the same thing Mr. Folopoulos, the play director, said when he started a rehearsal. It means we have to start at the first lines of the play. I clapped my hands. "Wow! You sound just like a real director."

Connor looked happy when I said that.

See what I mean about being a very good big sister?

"Let's start at the part where Alice is chasing the White Rabbit."

"Okay," I said. "You pretend to be Alice."

He nodded. "Oh, flower, did you see a White Rabbit?"

"I did!" I pretended my arms were leaves and waved them excitedly.

Connor frowned. "Lark, you're a flower. They're soft, so you should be too. You should whisper your line instead of shouting it. And I don't think you should wave your arms so much. You look like you're in a hurricane or something."

Hmm, he had a good point. "Okay, I won't wave my arms so much, but I have to be loud. If I'm not, the audience won't hear me."

"Yes, they will. You are very loud even when you're trying to be quiet."

"Connor!"

"See? Very loud."

Ugh. Little brothers. "Anyway, I decided I'm a Venus flytrap. They're carniv—carnival—" I couldn't remember the word. "They're plants that hunt bugs and eat them. So I don't have to be soft."

He shrugged. "Okay. Let's try again. Oh, flower, did you see a White Rabbit?"

"He went to the left!" Dramatically, I pointed to the left. Only I may have been a little too dramatic. My hand hit the lamp, and it crashed to the floor. That scared Max. He jumped off the couch and ran away. Only he caught his paw in the lamp cord and dragged it along with him. The cord got wrapped around the table leg, and everything went crashing to the ground. *Thump! Boom! Smash!*

Connor and I looked at each other. A few seconds later we heard the creak of a bedroom door opening, then the sound of footsteps on the stairs.

I held my breath.

So did Connor.

Mom and Dad can be kind of grumpy in the morning.

The footsteps got closer, and closer, and closer. It was Halmoni! She's never grumpy with us. Which is amazing, because Connor can really bring out the grumps!

She looked at us and smiled. "It's time to take a break for breakfast. What do you think?"

Chapter Two

Halmoni is Dad's mom. *Babu*—that's Swahili for *grandfather*—is Mom's dad. He is in Kenya, counting elephants. Halmoni let us video-chat with him while we had breakfast. Babu ate *mandazi* and we ate apple cinnamon pancakes, and we talked about elephants.

Connor and I also told Babu about our mystery-solving adventures. This summer we had already solved two cases!

That made us private investigators, or P.I.s. Our detective agency had a name and everything. Lark and Connor Ba's Detective Agency. We even had a mascot. It was an alligator because I love them. Plus, *alligator* rhymes with *investigator*, and I really like that!

Babu was very proud of us.

I was proud of us too.

We finished our breakfast, then helped Halmoni clean up the kitchen.

Then it was time for us to go to the playhouse.

"I'm getting more and more excited. I've never been in a play before!" I said.

Halmoni laughed. "I can see—you're beside yourself!"

I frowned. It was impossible for me to be beside myself. Plus, it was Connor who was beside me, but I didn't say anything. I didn't want to hurt Halmoni's feelings.

Halmoni locked the door, and then we were off to the rehearsals. We walked and talked, and in no time at all we were at the playhouse.

I grabbed Halmoni's hand. "This is so exciting. I have butterflies in my stomach!"

She squeezed my fingers. "Me too. Come on. Let's go inside and see what's happening."

We walked past the ticket booth and through the main doors. Miss Balza stood in front of us. I like her a lot! She has curly hair and it's the color of a sunset. I think she's very lucky because she has ~~freckls~~, ~~freakills~~, freckles. Today she didn't seem very lucky. Today she seemed very unlucky because her face was all frowny and sad. I did not like that at all. Nope, nope, nope.

Chapter Three

"Miss Balza," I asked, "are you okay? You don't look very happy."

"I don't feel very happy," she said, "but now you and Connor are here, and that makes me feel better. I heard about how the two of you helped Mrs. Robinson find the lost library. And how you helped Mr. and Mrs. Lee find out who stole the diamond earrings from their store." She bent down in front of us. "I'd like to hire the two of you."

I squeezed Connor's hands. This was so exciting—our third case. "Sure thing," I said. "What's the problem?"

"Someone has been playing pranks on the theater," she said. "I need you to help me find the culprit."

A culprit is someone who is responsible for doing something naughty. I liked that word a lot, but now wasn't the time to say that to Miss Balza.

"We can help," said Connor.

"Thank you so much!" She smiled a big, cheery smile.

One of the things I have learned about being a detective and solving a mystery is to get all the facts of the crime. "Miss Balza, could you please tell us what happened?"

"The first day of rehearsals, everything was fine. The trouble began on day two. Some of the props for the set were moved. And on day three, someone stapled the curtains shut. Yesterday the lightbulbs for the makeup table went missing. And today I found that someone had cut all the buttons off the costumes." She sighed a heavy sigh. "It gets worse. Mr. Folopoulos said if we can't stop the pranks, he's going to shut down the play."

"That's terrible," said Halmoni. "Everyone's working so hard."

"Can you think of anyone who would want to play these pranks?" asked Connor.

That was a good question, and it leads to the second thing I've learned about being a P.I. A person needs a *motive*. That's a reason for doing what they did.

Miss Balza shook her head. "No. Everyone here is so nice and helpful."

"Not everyone," I said. "Someone here is playing pranks."

"We should start with a list of everyone who is part of the play," said Connor.

"We can check the master list in the office. It has everyone's names and their jobs." Miss Balza looked at Connor and said, "Oh my goodness! Connor, I'm so sorry! You need to be on stage in five minutes, not helping me." Miss Balza looked at her clipboard. "Lark, you're not onstage until this afternoon."

"That's good," I said. "That means I have all morning to investigate."

"I can investigate too," Connor said. "I can watch from the stage and see if anyone is acting strange. Lark, when you're done talking to Miss Balza, you can check around the theater for anything that seems suspicious."

"That's a great plan," I told him. "Good luck with rehearsal!"

"Thanks," he said and headed up to the stage.

Miss Balza and I went to her office to find her papers. We walked past my friends Franklin and Kate. They were with Loi. She babysits us when Mom, Dad and Halmoni go out. I really like her. She's a teenager and in junior high, and she's great at everything! Franklin, Kate and Loi were sitting in a circle, practicing their lines. I noticed they were making notes on their scripts with different-colored pens, like pink, purple, green, blue, red and black. What a great idea! When I saw Connor, I was going to

tell him that was something we should do too.

I went into the office and said to Miss Balza, "Maybe someone is mad because they didn't get a part. Do you have anything like that in your notes?"

"Hmm. Do you know Sophie?" she asked.

I nodded. Sophie is in my class. We are best friends—she just doesn't know it yet.

"She tried out for the part of Alice, but Loi got it instead. Mrs. Wiedman auditioned for the role of the White Rabbit, but that went to Connor. Mr. Lee auditioned for the role of the Mad Hatter, but that went to Liam. Mrs. Wiedman, Mr. Lee and Sophie are the understudies," said Miss Balza. "That means if Loi, Liam or Connor can't perform, Sophie,

Mr. Lee and Mrs. Wiedman would get to play those roles."

"That's a good motive for getting rid of Loi and Liam and Connor," I said, "but not such a good motive for pranks."

"That's a good point." She sighed.

"I should still double-check," I said. I took out my detective notebook and wrote down their names. I have dyslexia. Which means letters and numbers can get mixed up in my head. Writing takes me a little longer, but I know if I'm patient I can do it.

Miss Balza's phone beeped—and kept beeping. "Oh! That's my alarm. Mr. Lee is bringing our morning snack, and he's bringing hot dogs for lunch. I have to go or I'll be late!"

She ran to find Mr. Lee and help with the food. Miss Balza had a job to do, and so did I. It was time to find the prankster.

Chapter Four

After Miss Balza left I went to the side of the stage so I could watch the actors rehearse and keep an eye on the people backstage. Connor did a great job of being the rabbit. Franklin did an equally great job of playing a mulberry bush. And the other person onstage was Loi. She had *a lot* of lines. She forgot some of them and got some of her words mixed up, but I thought she did great too.

I took out my detective notebook and wrote down everything I saw. Which wasn't a lot.

Halmoni left her lighting group to talk to Principal Robinson, who was one of the set builders.

Miss Balza and Mr. Lee put trays of fruits and pastries on a table.

Loi asked if she could get a drink of water from the fountain.

Mrs. Wiedman asked Franklin to try on a vest she was making for his costume.

Mr. Folopoulos called a break for a snack.

Connor saw me and waved me over. "Did you notice anything?" he asked.

I shook my head no. "Did you?"

He shook his head. "Me neither. Maybe we'll think better after a snack," he said. "I can't believe we don't have any suspects."

"We kind of do." I told him about Mrs. Wiedman and Sophie and Mr. Lee.

"That's a good list," said Connor, "and I'm not surprised Sophie's on it. I bet she's the culprit. She's always in trouble for something."

"We shouldn't jump to conclusions," I said. That meant we shouldn't make decisions about who was guilty before we had all the evidence.

"I guess, but I still think Sophie's involved. Come on. Let's go get our snack."

When we got to the table, we saw Franklin and Kate. Franklin handed me a cup of juice. "This acting thing is challenging."

"And it makes your throat dry," added Kate.

"Is that why you're holding two cups of juice?" I asked as I pointed at her hands.

She laughed. "No. Loi went to the bathroom. I'm holding her juice until she comes back." Then she looked at her fingers. "I'm going to have to go and wash my hands too. We were using her pens to make notes on our scripts, but they leak."

"I saw you making notes," I told her. "You should do that too, Connor. It will help you be a better actor."

He sighed and took a sip of his juice.

"I'm having lots of fun," said Franklin. "You were standing all by yourself, Lark. Are you bored?"

"Not even a little bit! It's fun to watch everyone practice. Not just the actors either. It's cool watching how the lights change and stuff. Plus, Connor, I was paying lots of attention to you. I have all kinds of ideas for you to make your part better."

He sighed louder and took another sip of his juice.

A couple of seconds later Loi joined our group. "Thanks for holding my juice," she said to Kate. "But on second thought, I better not have any. I heard sugar can be bad for your voice. Maybe I should stick to water." She lifted her water bottle, and her charm bracelet jingled.

"Is that new?" I asked. "It's pretty."

She nodded. "I was telling my auntie about the play and how nervous I felt. She bought it for me. It has charms of some of my most favorite things—a dog, a cat, a soccer ball and a microscope.

She says it's good luck, and I'll definitely break a leg if I wear it."

Connor frowned. "Why would she want to break a leg?" he whispered.

"Wouldn't that mean she doesn't get to go onstage?"

"Her aunt doesn't *really* want her to break a leg. It's what grown-ups in the theater say to wish each other good luck."

"Oh." He nodded. "I get it now." He frowned. "No, I don't. Grown-ups are weird."

"Are you guys having fun?" Loi asked.

We nodded.

"Are you?" I asked her.

She thought for a minute. "Yes, but it's a lot harder than it looks," she said. "I know my lines in my head, but it's a lot tougher when you have to say them out loud. And it's hard doing it in front of people. I wish we had more time to practice, but the opening night is just a few weeks away. I wish I wasn't so nervous."

She shook her bracelet, and it made a happy, twinkly sound. "Good thing I have this."

"Try practicing in front of a mirror," I said, "or recording yourself. That can be helpful." I turned to Connor. "We should do that with you."

"I can't wait until you have to get up there," Connor said. "I'm going to make sure Halmoni records you."

"Thank you." I patted his hand. "That will be very helpful."

He sighed and rolled his eyes. "I was being sarcastic, Lark."

Little brothers. They can be so confusing, even when you're trying to give them a compliment.

Mr. Folopoulos called everyone back to work on the next scene.

Connor didn't have to be onstage.

That meant he could keep going with our investigation. "See you later. I hope you break an arm and a leg!"

Loi's face puckered in confusion.

"He means good luck," I told her.

"Oh." She smiled. "Thanks, Connor!"

Just as our friends left, Mrs. Robinson came up to us.

"I'm part of the scenery team," she said. "We are going outside and painting the flowers." She held up red and green paint cans. "I know how much you and Connor like painting and how good you both are at it. Maybe you'd like to help paint the stems and leaves?"

Painting scenery sounded like so much fun. But we had a job to do. "We'd like to, Mrs. Robinson, but we're helping Miss Balza with a project right now."

"Okay," she said. "I'll put it aside. At lunch I'll ask Miss Balza about you helping with the painting."

"That sounds great. Thanks."

"Where should we start?" asked Connor after Mrs. Robinson had left. "We watched everyone before snack time and didn't see anything."

"Maybe we should investigate the places where the pranks happened," I suggested.

He nodded. "That's a great idea. There might be a clue. Let's start looking."

Chapter Five

We climbed the steps to the stage and went to the left, to where the makeup tables were set up. Miss Balza was right. Each table had a mirror attached to it, and there was a light fixture attached to each mirror. But the lightbulbs were missing.

"I wish I had a fingerprint kit," said Connor. "We could dust for fingerprints. Then we could take fingerprints of everyone in the play and compare them. We'd find the prankster for sure!"

"Yes," I said, "but that would take a long time. Plus, the ink would make everyone's hands dirty. They'd have to wash and wash, and that would take even more time. It was a good idea though."

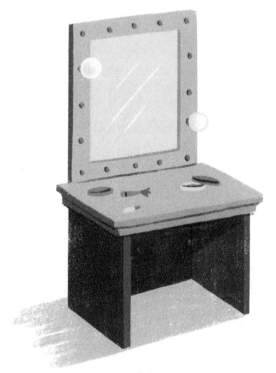

"Maybe the culprit dropped something, like a store receipt. The detective in the mystery book I borrowed from the library found the bad guy because of some thread he found on the ground."

"That's a great idea!" We searched around, but it was all bad news. There was nothing on the makeup tables. They were all neat and tidy, except for a couple of blue smears.

Connor poked one of the smears. "I think that's the makeup for the Caterpillar."

"Maybe we'll have better luck with the curtains."

But we didn't. There weren't any clues. The area around the curtains was just as clean as the area around the makeup tables.

"The custodian, Mr. Lancaster, must have cleaned up," I said.

"I feel terrible," said Connor. "We've been looking forever, but we aren't any closer to figuring out who the prankster is!"

I felt bad too. I felt...it started with a *d* or maybe a *j*, and it was a good word that meant I felt extra sad. "Maybe we need a breath of fresh air. That will help clear our minds."

He nodded. "That's not a bad idea. Let's take a break from investigating the scenes of the crimes. I think we should talk to our suspects next."

"That is a good idea," I said, "but we should act like we don't *think* they're suspects."

We went outside. There was a group of people painting the set flowers.

The flowers were red and blue and pink and purple. Sophie was in the group.

"There's our number-one suspect," Connor said quietly.

She stopped painting when she saw us. "Baa baa Lark sheep."

I laughed.

Connor growled.

He doesn't like that joke, and he thinks Sophie's mean. But I think the joke is funny because my last name is Ba and *baa* is the sound sheep make. "Hello, Sophie," I said as we walked over.

Connor stared at her. "Have you been eating paint?"

"That's dangerous!" She glared at him. "I wouldn't do something like that."

"Then why are your teeth and face all blue?"

"I had blueberries with my breakfast," she said. "My *babushka* is visiting, and we've been baking all kinds of yummy things with blueberries. They're my favorite fruit. I even brought some as a snack. They're tasty, but they stain."

"Baking things with blueberries sounds like a delicious thing to do," I said.

"It is, but we're running out of things to make." She peered at us. "Why are you here? Not to talk to me about blueberries, that's for sure."

I told her about the pranks.

She scowled. "Do you think I did something? Is that why you came over?"

"No. Not even a little bit."

"Good, because I didn't do any of it."

"Have you seen anything strange?" asked Connor.

"Just you," she said.

He made a frowny, growly face at her.

"What about when you were on a break?" I asked.

She scowled again. "I'm too busy to take a break," she said. "Everyone is. It's a lot of work putting on a play."

"That's too bad." I sighed. "I was hoping you could help. The play might get shut down if we can't figure out who's playing the pranks."

She sighed too. "That is terrible. My babushka was going to watch rehearsals with me tomorrow. I get to be onstage because Loi has a dentist appointment. I've been practicing really, really hard." She made a grumpy face. "You better solve this, Lark sheep!"

"I'm going to do my best," I said.

Connor growled. "*We're* going to do our best."

"Good." Sophie went back to her painting.

"This is terrible," said Connor as we walked away. "It's almost lunch, and we don't know anything."

"Let's check the costumes," I said. "Miss Balza said someone had cut the buttons off some of them."

The dressing room held lots of things that could be clues. And that made me so happy! There were boxes of costumes and racks of costumes. On the floor we found a penny, a dime and a quarter. We found a receipt from Lee's General Store. We also found ~~seekwins~~, ~~seQuinns~~, sequins, a black sock, some metal clips and a long string of black thread.

"Look at all this stuff," Connor said excitedly. "I bet something here is a clue!"

Just then Franklin ran up to us. "Come on, guys! It's lunchtime, and Mr. Lee brought hot dogs!"

"Hot dogs! I'm going to have mine with mustard and onions *and* relish," said Connor. He ran off with Franklin.

I wanted to run too, but something shiny caught my eye. Not really. That would really hurt my eye. Something *catching my eye* means that something caught my attention. I went over to the shiny thing on the floor and picked it up. And I did not like what it was. Not one little bit. Nope, nope, nope.

Chapter Six

I found Connor in the lineup for lunch.
"I have to talk to you," I said. "I found
a clue, and you're not going to like it."

We went to a quiet spot and I showed
him what I'd found. "It's a microscope
charm. I think it's from Loi's bracelet."

"Oh, man." Connor looked sad.
"You're right. I don't like that."

"Me neither. But we'll have to talk
to her."

We found Loi on the stage, reading over her script and making notes with her blue pen. "Hi, guys," she said, smiling. "Lark, I know we're supposed to rehearse your scenes after lunch, but I'm nervous about the stuff we did this morning. I asked Mr. Folopoulos if we could do a run-through with just my lines after lunch. Is that okay with you?"

I nodded. "We have to ask you something."

"Sure. Is everything okay? What's going on?"

I told her about the pranks.

"We've been investigating the spots where the pranks happened," said Connor. He showed her the microscope charm. "And we found this."

Her eyes went wide. "My charm! Oh my goodness!" She grabbed both of us and hugged us hard. "I lost two of them this morning, and I've been looking all over for them! Did you find the soccer ball too?"

I shook my head no.

"Come on! Let's tell Mrs. Wiedman!" She jumped up and ran over to the costume area.

Connor and I followed.

"Mrs. Wiedman! Mrs. Wiedman!"

"Yes?" Mrs. Wiedman stood up from the chair. "What's going on?"

"Lark and Connor found my microscope charm!"

"What a relief!" said Mrs. Wiedman. "I was looking for them for you."

"Where did you find it?" Loi asked me.

"With the costumes."

"I was trying on the Alice costume this morning with Mrs. Wiedman. It must have fallen off when I took off the dress. I'm so glad you found it! I was worried I'd lost it for good."

"You should go and see one of the set designers," said Mrs. Wiedman. "I bet they'll have the tools to fit the charm back on your bracelet."

"That's a great idea," said Loi.

She sped off.

"I bet the soccer ball is in those clothes somewhere too," said Mrs. Wiedman. "I'll keep looking. Good work, you two."

"I'm glad that got explained," said Connor. "I would have been sad if the prankster was Loi."

"Me too," I said.

Connor and I told Mrs. Wiedman about the pranks. "We don't think you did those things," said Connor. "But have you seen anything suspicious?"

"No, I'm sorry," she said. "I've been so busy making the costumes, I'm afraid I don't notice anything but needle, thread and cloth. If I see anything suspicious, I'll tell you."

We thanked her, then went back to where everyone was gathered for lunch. They were outside in the sunshine. Mr. Lee had set up a bunch of tables.

"Mr. Lee is one of our suspects," said Connor. "We should talk to him too."

We told Mr. Lee about the pranks.

"We don't think you did those things," said Connor, "but maybe you saw something?"

He shook his head sadly. "No, I'm sorry. I just drop off the food, and then I go straight back to the store. I haven't seen anything unusual."

"Thank you," I said.

"Have a hot dog," he said. "Maybe some food will help."

We got our lunch and went to where Franklin and Kate sat. I put my book on one of the seats to save it for Sophie.

"I think I took too much fruit," said Loi as she sat down beside Connor with a plate piled high. "You're welcome to share it with me." She held the plate out, and her bracelet went *tinkle, tinkle*. "Look, it's all fixed!"

"Don't you like hot dogs?" asked Connor.

"I love them," she said, "but the fruit looked so delicious, I couldn't resist."

"Mr. Lee said you and Connor helped him find earrings that were stolen from their store," said Loi.

"That's true." Connor's chest went all puffy because he was proud. "We did."

"Tell me everything."

Connor and I took turns telling Loi about our adventure. When he talked, I ate. When I talked, he ate. As we were talking, Sophie came to our table. She added in stuff too. When we were done, Loi leaned back and said, "Wow. You two are good detectives."

"Not that great," said Connor. "I lost a pickle." He lifted his plate and checked underneath. "Not there."

I pointed at Loi's hand. "Right now I detect you have ketchup on your fingers."

She laughed. "Guilty. I better go wash up." Loi grabbed my hand and squeezed. "Thanks again for finding my charm. That was great of you!" She walked away.

"I'm going to get another hot dog," said Sophie.

Just as she left, Miss Balza and Halmoni came up.

"Lark," said Miss Balza, "do you remember Mrs. Robinson asking you about painting the flowers?"

"Yes."

"Well..." She glanced at Halmoni. "I was wondering if maybe you had decided to help with the painting."

"No," I said.

Connor shook his head. "Me neither."

"Oh." She gave Halmoni another look. This time she seemed worried.

Chapter Seven

"Is everything okay?" asked Connor.

"Halmoni will explain," said Miss Balza. "I have to go and find Mr. Folopoulos. Excuse me."

"Someone has played another prank on the theater—with the wooden flowers," said Halmoni as Miss Balza walked away. "Miss Balza and I were painting them purple and red. I checked on the flowers five minutes ago, and they were there.

But when I walked by just now, they were gone! Plus, someone got something blue all over some of the costumes. We can't wash it off, so they'll have to be sent out for dry cleaning."

Crickets! More pranks!

"That's terrible," said Connor.

Halmoni stood up. "Yes, but I know if you put your heads together, you'll figure it out." She smiled and walked away.

I smiled too, but I was confused.

So was Connor. "How will putting our heads together help?"

"I don't know," said Franklin. "But maybe you should try it."

Connor and I tilted our heads so our foreheads touched.

"Did you figure out anything?" I asked.

"Only where my lost pickle is," said Connor. "I dropped it on my lap."

I sighed and pulled away. "This is our hardest case yet!"

"Baa baa Lark sheep." Sophie stood at our table with a plate of food in her hand. "Did you solve the case yet?"

I shook my head.

"And there's been another prank— two of them!" said Connor.

"I thought you guys were great detectives," she said. "I thought you would have solved it by now."

"Me too," I said.

She picked up her hot dog and bit into it.

Connor nudged me, and I knew why.

Sophie's hands were all blue.

Chapter Eight

Connor and I moved to a quiet spot where no one could hear us talk.

"There was blue stuff on the costumes, and Sophie's hands are blue," said Connor. "I think she's the culprit, Lark."

Double crickets! I couldn't believe that was true! "But it doesn't make sense. Why would she play those pranks?"

"Because Sophie always trouble."

"Not always."

"Fine." He sighed. "But she causes trouble *a lot.*"

"But what's her motive?" I asked. "Why would she do all this stuff?"

He shrugged. "Maybe she was mad because she didn't get the role of Alice."

"Maybe," I said, "but she didn't seem angry. She said she wanted us to solve the case."

"Maybe she was just acting," said Connor. "When I was the weeping willow, I pretended there was a breeze when there wasn't any. Maybe she was pretending she was happy even though she didn't feel happy."

Maybe. Sophie *was* a good actor.

"We should tell Mr. Folopoulos and Miss Balza."

"What if we're wrong? We could get Sophie into a lot of trouble, and she doesn't deserve that."

"All the evidence points to her," Connor said. "The blue stuff. Plus, when the flowers went missing, Sophie was the only one who wasn't at our table."

"I don't know."

"You heard what Miss Balza said. If we don't catch the prankster, the play gets canceled. We have to tell her what we know."

"Give me ten minutes to think about it," I pleaded. "And if I can't think of another suspect, then we'll talk to Miss Balza, okay?"

He sighed. "Okay, but only ten minutes."

I went and sat under one of the trees. This was terrible. Not only had Connor and I missed another prank, but now the play was going to *not* be a play anymore. And my best friend, Sophie, might be the one responsible for this mess! My bestest day was turning into my worstest day.

Chapter Nine

This was a really hard mystery. There were a lot of people, a lot of places and a lot of things to keep track of. My brain felt confused, and my heart felt worried because I didn't want to let anyone down. I closed my eyes and listened to the wind.

I thought really hard about the case. I took out my notebook and flipped it open. Then I wrote what I knew so far.

1. Someone is playing pranks.

2. That someone has to have a motive.

3. The play is going to be shut down if the pranks continue.

4. People are going to be very sad if the play is shut down

5. The prankster is going to be happy if the play is shut down.

I tapped my pencil against my chin. I wasn't sure how the prankster would feel, so I made a change.

5. The prankster is MAYBE going to be happy if the play is shut down.

6. Someone has taken the light bulbs, moved the props, cut off the buttons from the costumes, removed the wooden flowers, stapled the curtains together and left blue stains on some of the costumes.

That was better. Now I could see everything I needed to see. But there were still lots of questions in my brain.

Why would the prankster want to shut down the play? And why were they pulling so many different pranks? I closed my eyes and thought of how hard everybody was working. And I kept my eyes closed and thought of the prankster. They were working hard too—but in a bad way.

When I had talked to Miss Balza, we'd thought maybe the prankster was mad. But no one seemed mad. Not even Sophie. Maybe the prankster had a different feeling. I thought of all the reasons someone might want the play to shut down. Maybe they were afraid they would get hurt because of all the stuff going on. They could cut themselves building the set. They could fall off a ladder. They could forget their lines. They could forget to turn the lights on or off.

Then I thought about where everyone had been during the day. Halmoni had been working on the lights. Kate, Franklin and Loi had been on stage. Miss Balza had been all over the place. Mr. Folopoulos had been in one of the theater seats.

Then I thought about everything I had seen at the scenes of the pranks. I wrote down those things too. We had found Loi's charm, a penny, blue makeup, a dime, a quarter, a receipt, sequins, a black sock, some metal clips and a long string of black thread.

I looked at all the things I had written down. And I looked at my hand, holding the pencil. Then I closed my eyes and thought, and then I thought some more.

My eyes snapped open. I knew who the culprit was but it didn't make me very happy.

Chapter Ten

I jumped up from the ground and ran for the theater door. It flew open and Connor ran out. He held up his paper. "I thought about what you said, about how Sophie might not be the culprit. And I thought about the blue stuff we'd seen on the makeup table, and the blue stuff Halmoni said was on the costumes."

"You thought it was blueberry juice."

He nodded. "At first we thought it was makeup. Then we thought it was blueberry juice. But then I started thinking about acting and pretending and the prankster's motive," he said. "And we thought maybe the person was angry—"

"But they're not angry," I said. "They're scared."

"Right," said Connor. "At lunch, when we were talking to Loi—"

"—she had the red stuff on her hands."

"Right," he said. "And you said she had ketchup on her hands. But she was eating fruit, so it couldn't have been ketchup."

"It wasn't," I said sadly. "If it had been ketchup, then when she grabbed my hand I would've gotten ketchup

on my fingers. But it was dried paint."
I held up my hand. "That's why my
hands don't have anything on them.
Halmoni and Miss Balza were painting
the flowers. They must have still been
wet when Loi moved them."

"Kate said she was using Loi's pens
and they had left ink on her fingers.
That's the blue stuff. Not makeup or
blueberry juice, but ink."

I nodded. "The prankster is Loi."

"This doesn't make me feel good,"
he said. "I like Loi, and I don't want to
get her in trouble."

"Me either, but we made a promise to Halmoni and Miss Balza." I thought of Sophie. "Plus, there's a whole bunch of people who deserve to have the play go on. What Loi did wasn't right. And we almost got Sophie in trouble."

He nodded. "Let's go talk to Halmoni and Miss Balza."

Chapter Eleven

We found Halmoni and Miss Balza and told them what we thought. Miss Balza called Loi over. As soon as she saw us, Loi said, "It was at lunch, wasn't it? You saw the paint."

"I thought it was ketchup," said Connor.

"Plus the blue stuff on the costumes," I said. "The prankster didn't play the same trick twice. It was the makeup table, then the costumes, then the flowers. It didn't make sense for the prankster to play another trick with the costumes. So why did you go back?"

"I wanted to see if my soccer-ball charm was there," she said.

"And you got blue ink on the clothes."

"Loi, why would you do something like this?" asked Halmoni.

She started to cry. "I thought I could manage the role of Alice and it would be fun. But it is so much harder than I thought. No matter how much I practice, I can't remember my lines. And I got scared. I thought of what would happen if I forgot my lines onstage with everyone watching."

"But your pranks are going to cost the theater money—not to mention all the delays," said Miss Balza.

"I'm so sorry." Loi cried harder. "I wasn't trying to be mean or make anyone mad. I only wanted to get more time. I didn't think Mr. Folopoulos would shut down the play."

"We're going to have to talk to your parents," said Miss Balza. "And I'm not sure if Mr. Folopoulos or the other folks in the theater will want you to be part of the play anymore."

"I'm sorry," Loi said again. "And I'm really sorry to you guys. I know it was hard to tell Halmoni and Miss Balza. I'm sorry I let you down."

"You didn't let me down," said Connor.

"Me neither," I said. "I just wish you had told somebody you were scared instead of playing pranks."

"I didn't know how to ask for more time," she said. "And I was scared everyone would be mad because they thought I was letting them down." The tears fell down her face. "But it doesn't matter because they'll still be mad at me."

"I'm not mad at you," I said. "I feel sad."

"Me too," said Connor.

Loi left with Halmoni and Miss Balza.

"Will you tell me if you're afraid of anything?" asked Connor.

"I promise. Will you?"

"Yes."

A little while later Loi, Mr. Folopoulos, Miss Balza, Loi's parents and Halmoni came onstage. Loi explained what she'd done and why, and she apologized. Then Mr. Folopoulos said, "Loi will pay for the dry cleaning. She will also fix the makeup tables and help sew the buttons back on the costumes. But in regard to her being part of the play, I thought we would leave it to you to decide."

I raised my hand. "I'm okay with her being part of the play. She said sorry, and she meant it."

"Plus, she's fixing her mistakes," Connor added. "I'm okay with her staying on."

The rest of the folks in the theater agreed.

"Because there should be a consequence for what Loi did," said Mr. Folopoulos, "she will split her part with Sophie. Half of the time, Sophie will be Alice. The other half of the time, Loi will be Alice."

"Wow!" Sophie said. "That's cool! My babushka will get to see me perform!"

Halmoni came off the stage, and I went to see her.

"That was a good job you did," she said. "It took excellent observational skills to realize the red stains on her hands were paint and not ketchup. And it was very clever to realize the blue smudges were ink."

"Thanks," I said, "but I don't feel very happy."

"Oh," she said. "Why not?"

"I like Loi, and I didn't like getting her in trouble."

"First of all," said Halmoni, "Loi got herself in trouble, not you. But I know how you feel. I like Loi too, and

I didn't like seeing her get into trouble either. Sometimes doing the right thing isn't the same as doing the easy thing. But I'm very proud of all three of you. You and Connor told us what you discovered. Loi apologized and will work to fix her mistake.

"I think now more than ever Loi could use a friend." Halmoni smiled at me. "And I bet if you got a chance to talk to her, and help her with her feelings, you'll get that happy feeling for having done the right thing."

Chapter Twelve

The next morning Loi, Connor and I knocked on Sophie's door.

"Baa baa Lark sheep," she said when she opened the door and saw us. "What do you guys want?"

Loi held out her hand. "I wanted to say I'm doubly sorry to you. I didn't think the blue smudges might look like blueberry juice. I almost got you in trouble for something I did."

Sophie shrugged and took Loi's hand. "Thanks, I guess."

"I wonder if you might practice with me? Maybe I'll remember the lines better with your help?" Loi asked.

"Of course you will," said Sophie. "I'm a great actor and an excellent teacher." She looked at Connor and me. "Why are you two here?"

"Connor and I are going to the library this afternoon. Would you like to come with us?"

"Why would I go to the library?"

"Because you said you and your babushka had run out of things to make with blueberries. If we go to the library, I bet we can find a book with all sorts of things you can do with blueberries."

"Hmm." She thought for a minute. "Okay, Lark sheep. That's a great idea.

I'll come to your house later and we can go to the library."

I grinned. This really was the bestest day ever!

THE WORDS LARK LOVES

CHAPTER ONE:

"Anyway, I decided I'm a Venus flytrap. They're carniv—carnival—" I couldn't remember the word. "They're plants that hunt bugs and eat them. So I don't have to be soft."

This awesome word is *carnivorous*, and it's a word used to describe an animal or plant that eats meat. For example, the dinosaur *Tyrannosaurus rex* ate other dinosaurs, and that made him a carnivorous animal.

CHAPTER FIVE:

I felt...it started with a d *or maybe a* j, *and it was a good word that meant I felt extra sad.*

The word Lark was thinking of is *dejected*. It's a super-great word that means you're feeling really, really sad. For Lark, not being able to solve the case left her feeling dejected.

THE STUFF LARK *ALMOST* GOT RIGHT

CHAPTER TWO:
Halmoni laughed. "I can see—you're beside yourself!"

That would be impossible. Being *beside yourself* means being extremely happy! When Lark gets to be part of the play, she's so excited and happy that she's beside herself.

CHAPTER SEVEN:

"Yes, but I know if you put your heads together, you'll figure it out."

Halmoni didn't mean for Lark and Connor to actually put their heads together. *Putting your heads together* means working as a team, trading ideas and trying to come up with the solution to a problem together.

ACKNOWLEDGMENTS

Thanks to my fabulous editor, Liz Kemp. Her suggestions make Lark and Connor's adventures so much better. My gratitude as well to the entire Orca pod for being so wonderful and for all their efforts with the series. Finally, thank you to Marcus Cutler for his amazing illustrations.

Award-winning author **NATASHA DEEN** loves stories—exciting ones, scary ones and, especially, funny ones! Her most recent stories include *Lark Holds the Key* (starred selection, CCBC Best Books for Kids & Teens), *Terminate* and *Across the Floor* (starred selection, CCBC Best Books for Kids & Teens). When she's not working on her books or visiting schools and libraries, she spends a lot of time trying to convince her dogs and cats that she's the boss of the house. Visit her at natashadeen.com.